DIRTY SOCKS DON'T WIN GAMES

Other books you will enjoy by DEAN MARNEY

The Computer That Ate My Brother

You, Me, and Gracie Makes Three

The Trouble with Jake's Double

DIRTY SOCKS DON'T WIN GAMES

Dean Marney

AN
APPLE
PAPERBACK

SCHOLASTIC INC.
New York Toronto London Auckland Sydney

ISBN 0-590-44880-3

Copyright © 1992 by Dean Marney.
All rights reserved. Published by Scholastic Inc.
APPLE PAPERBACKS is a registered trademark of Scholastic Inc.

12 11 10 9 8 7 6 5 4 3   2 3 4 5 6 7 8/9

Printed in the U.S.A.   2 8

First Scholastic printing, August 1992

DIRTY SOCKS DON'T WIN GAMES

Time-out
The Boys' Team

Brent's Story: *How did I get us into this? Hey, we love sports, but playing a girls' team in a basketball tournament? No way. Well, maybe if we can find a ladder to check their seven-foot center.*

1

Who are we? What planet did we come from? What are we doing here?

Try to care because I'm going to tell you anyway. We're wild. We're lean and mean. We're here to play. We're sports machines. People call us the Jocks.

Saying we like sports is a lie. We are closer to sports addicts. Having fun is something we take seriously.

I have been known to play hockey with a knife and the peas on my plate. Mashed potatoes make good goals. I was asked to leave the table once for trying to teach a string bean to do a one-and-a-half with a twist into my sister's milk. If I could have had one more try, the bean would have made it.

My mother hates it when anyone calls me a jock. She says, "It sounds like dirty underpants."

I say, "That's pretty strange, Mom."

The Jocks are a group of us. We're not a dumb

club. We're six guys who are friends and we love sports.

We live close together, easy biking distance. We're not all the same age. The thing that we have in common is that if there's a sport we've done it or we're going to do it.

My name is Brent. I'm the next Michael Jordan. I'm in the sixth grade and right now I "do" basketball. I think I'm pretty amazing. In fact, it's my motto: "Amaze them, make them stupid with your moves."

I don't know exactly why but I've got this thing for basketball. I even get excited when I smell the inside of my shoes. My mom caught me sniffing them and told me that if I did it again she'd burn them.

She said, "That's disgusting."

My mom just doesn't understand.

The only problem I have with basketball right now is that I'm not exactly a consistent shooter. I make up for it by being a great ball handler. I've got moves even I don't know about. I'm not lying, I handle the ball like most people handle breakfast . . . sort of.

I just thought of this guy I was checking once. He had this cold that was making all this snot run out his nose. I have never seen anyone let that much snot come out their nose at one time.

I said to him, "Hey, jerk, you're making me sick. Go blow your stupid nose."

4

You know what he did? He stuck out his tongue and licked clear up into his nostrils. Then the sucker smiled at me.

I was puking. I was gagging so hard they had to call a time-out. I couldn't believe the ref didn't throw him out. He just handed him a piece of toilet paper and told him to blow. Don't you just hate people who eat boogers?

2

Kent is pretty much my best friend. He's one of the Jocks. He's in the seventh grade.

We sometimes call him Clark Kent. He's into bodybuilding. His dad is really into it. His dad is huge.

Kent knows all this stuff about muscles from his dad. He's always talking about his gluts and his delts and his pecs. He can do more ab crunches than anyone I know.

He eats health food, too. He loses control when I try to get him to eat candy. He and Joel are alike when it comes to food.

Joel calls his body a perfectly designed sports car.

He says, "You wouldn't think of putting junk in a Lamborghini, would you? You'd put in only the best fuel possible. My body is a Lamborghini, and it only gets the best."

They both try really hard not to eat junk food. I've seen them slip though, but who can blame them. Sometimes you just have to have a candy bar.

When Joel sees me do it he says, "Hey, Brent buddy, I didn't know you were a dump truck."

Joel is also in the seventh grade. Maybe you start trying to eat healthy when you're in the seventh grade. I've got a little time. Maybe the school lunch is so bad you have to.

Joel is kind of weird. He's really into, like, setting goals and then he calls it making movies. He pictures himself doing his goals like they were actually happening in his head. When he's really into his head and he starts talking weird about it, you just want to bong him one.

There are three other guys in the Jocks. There's Gary. He's in the fifth grade and he's probably the fastest kid in the world. He's not very tall but you can't believe how fast this guy is. If he ran past you naked you wouldn't be able to tell it, he moves so fast.

Matt is in fifth grade, too. He's Mr. Kung Fu, martial artist. Some people give him crap because he has really long hair and wears it in a pony tail. I'm warning you, though, don't mess with him. I did only one time, and it was a major mistake.

The last guy in our group is Tony. He's in my grade, sixth. He thinks he's really hot-looking. He's always acting like he's hustling girls. Sometimes he totally embarrasses us.

When we're all together he'll yell at girls walking by.

Tony says things like, "He likes you. Hey, girl, he really really likes you." Then he'll point at one of us and say, "I mean it. He loves you. He wants to marry you."

At that point we have to kill him. We don't have a choice. It's too bad it doesn't do any good.

Here we are, the six of us: me, Kent, Joel, Gary, Matt, and Tony. We're the Jocks. If you've got a game, we want to be there . . . well, most of the time.

3

This tournament was kind of weird. It wasn't even basketball season anymore so not that many people had a team still going. They didn't have a tournament sponsor until a week before the thing.

That's when I found out about it. My dad brought over this really stupid-looking poster with a basketball with a clown face on it. He told me I should get the guys together and enter it.

I took a look at it and said, "No way."

My dad said, "That's too bad because my company is going to sponsor it, and I'm going to be an official scorekeeper."

I said, "Dad, even if I could get the guys all together we'd just barely have enough with six of us to stay alive in a tournament."

"I understand," he said. "I just thought it might be fun to watch you play."

I hate divorce. My dad has this look he gives me when I don't want to do something with him.

It kills me off. I think the zoo sucks but I keep going with him because he gives me that look.

"Dad," I said, "we wouldn't have a coach."

"George would do it," he said.

I was really sorry I had mentioned a coach. George is this guy at my dad's work who thinks he's a super coach but doesn't do anything. He's so weird.

Instead of telling you what offense to run or what's wrong with your defense or why you're shooting baskets like bricks, he tells you, "Pretend the basketball is square. Think about that."

"Dad, he's too weird."

"But he'd really enjoy it," my dad said.

"But even if we got him, we wouldn't have a sponsor for our team, and there isn't time to get shirts," I said.

"Well," said my dad, "I hope you won't be angry, but I asked your grandmother if she wouldn't like to sponsor you, and I rushed an order for T-shirts today."

"Really?" I said. "Dad, she owns an antique store. They don't usually sponsor teams."

"She liked the idea," said my dad. "She thought it would be interesting advertising."

"What do the T-shirts say?" I asked.

My dad laughed. "Let's have that be a surprise."

"I hate surprises," I said.

"You just get that team together."

10

"Dad, you know some of the guys really hate stupid-looking shirts."

"These are great," said my dad. "You'll love them."

"Dad, how will we find time to practice?" I said, but he didn't hear me. He was telling my mother that she was wrong and that I really wanted to be in this tournament.

I started calling the Jocks. Are these guys great or what? Joel, Gary, Matt, and Tony all said, "Sure, why not." Tony had a slight problem because he was grounded through Saturday for accidentally sticking his sister's Barbie in the garbage disposal. He was giving her a new hairdo. He thought he could work it off by cleaning the garage.

4

I went to Kent's house to tell him up front and personal that he was playing basketball for the weekend. He was outside in their garage doing what he loves best, pumping iron. He had his CD player just blaring.

"Don't mess up my concentration," he yelled. "You can't get big unless you concentrate."

I turned down the music.

"What are you doing?" he yelled at me, like the music was still really loud.

"I need to talk to you," I said, "and what's that smell?"

"What do you think of my rear deltoids? Do you think they're bigger?"

"Huge," I said. "How would I know? What is that smell? Did you have tofu for dinner?"

He threw his sweaty towel at me. "Jerk, you ruined my concentration."

"Listen, tuna melt," I said, "I have to talk to you about basketball."

"The season's over, it's my worst sport, and I can still beat you. What else is there that can be talked about?"

"Real funny," I said. "We're in a tournament this Saturday."

"You're in a tournament this Saturday. I'm going to the gym with my dad to do serious damage to my biceps."

"Kent," I said, "you have to do this for me. We have to have six guys at least. Even with six guys, if somebody fouls out we're going to be in major trouble."

"You got everyone else?" he asked.

"Ya," I said, picking up a dumbbell and jerking it over my head.

"Careful," he said, "it's heavier than you . . ."

He was trying to warn me, but it was too late. The weight was only above my head for a second and then it was throwing me backward toward the floor like I was a bridge. Kent zoomed over and tried to grab me or the weight or both of us, but by then it was too late. I pulled him over on top of me, clunking his head on some shelves full of tools.

With his knee in my face he said, "I don't think you should do backbends with heavy weights."

"Get off of me," I said. "I can't breathe. I wasn't doing a backbend, I was doing a one arm overhead press."

"It looked like a backbend to me," he said.

13

"It just turned out that way. Now I'm injured," I said, "and it's all your fault."

He was laughing. "You can't believe how stupid you looked. Are you okay? You have to be careful with weights. Start light and work up to heavy."

"Next time, for sure," I said. "I'm okay, really, if you hadn't've landed on me." Then we were both laughing.

"Saturday, huh," said Kent.

"Nine o'clock," I said.

"The Jocks strike again?" he said.

"We don't know how to stop."

5

We were all there Saturday morning. Of course, I was the first to arrive and Tony was the last one to show up.

He said, "Hey, I saw this really cute girl, but she must have been seven feet tall."

"Hey, Gary, you shrimp," said Joel, "she'd be just your size."

"Very funny," said Gary. "The doctor said I was soon going to hit a growth spurt and leave you guys behind."

"Right," said Tony.

"Hey, seriously," said Joel, "I heard about this guy who made himself taller by closing his eyes and seeing himself getting stretched taller and taller. It was like he was on a torture rack. He did it every night before he went to sleep. I mean, he, like, grew eight inches."

"Nah," said Tony, "I heard it was a girl, and she got bigger bazooms that way."

"Right," said Gary, "totally amazing but I don't want to hear about it."

"I was just trying to help," said Joel.

Matt, Mr. Kung Fu, was stretched out and doing some *katans*. They're like fake karate. It's karate, but you just do it by yourself. He was really red in the face.

"What's with the tomato face?" I asked him.

"I'm not red," said Matt.

"You're red," said Tony.

"Definitely crimson," said Joel.

"Hey, guy, you're a beet," said Gary.

"I've never seen anything redder," said Kent.

Matt just looked at us for a second.

"Fine," he said, "I went to the locker room over there and I walked in and there were a bunch of girls."

"Right," said Gary.

"No kidding," said Matt.

"What did you see?" said Tony.

"Nothing," said Matt, "they were all dressed."

"So why are you all red?" I asked.

"I told you I'm not," said Matt.

"Right," said Gary.

"Gary, you're beginning to tick me off," said Matt.

"Change the subject," I said.

"Where's our coach?" said Joel.

George was just walking over to us. He isn't much taller than we are and he was wearing funny shoes.

16

"Hey, guys," he said, "you ready to shoot some hoop?"

I looked at everyone. I knew they were like hating me because this guy is so weird. What could I have done?

"Yep, we are," I said. "Mr. — "

He interrupted me. "No, don't call me mister. Call me George or Uncle George."

I couldn't look at the guys or they'd be killing me.

"Uh, George, did you bring the T-shirts?" I asked.

"You bet," he said. He went over to the bleachers where there was a box and brought it back. "These are dynamite shirts, guys."

"They're tanks," said Tony. "I look like crap in a tank."

"I looked ripped in tanks," said Kent. "I love it."

Then Matt decided to ruin everything by proving he could read. "What does this mean?" he said.

"What?" I said.

" 'Get old at Granny's,' " he said. "It's on all the shirts."

"Get old at Granny's?" said Gary. "What does it mean?"

"It's a tough concept, guys," I said. "We're dealing with an antique store here. She sells old stuff, get it? She wants you to buy old stuff at her store."

They looked at me like I had hard-boiled-egg breath.

6

The Jocks were there. We looked great in our new tank T-shirts. Well, to tell the truth, we looked pretty stupid, but it wasn't anything we shouldn't have been able to overcome.

We shouldn't have cared what we looked like anyway. We were there to play basketball. It's the game of true athletes. It takes all skills: running, jumping, precision shooting, brilliant defense. We had the skills and we would put them together . . . maybe.

Uncle George (can you believe he said call me Uncle George) went over to see how we did on the draw. I was hoping he'd get lost on the way. It was a single elimination tournament, so unless we lost real fast we'd probably play three games to make it to the championship game.

We were playing regular rules except we were only going to play five-minute quarters. Even with halftime, the games would only last about a half hour. It didn't sound too tough to me.

Tony said, "Why didn't you get a pizza place to sponsor us? Why did you get your grandmother's antique shop?"

"Why do you care?" I said. "Let's just play basketball, okay?" I was getting sort of ticked off.

Then we saw this team of girls hit the floor.

"That's them," said Matt.

"There's the seven-foot wonder," said Tony.

"What are they doing here?" asked Joel.

"Is there a girl's tournament, too?" asked Kent.

"I don't think so," I said.

George came back. "It's great, guys," said George. "It's a piece of cake. Our first team is that one over there." He pointed to the girls' team.

We all stood there with our mouths hanging open.

I finally said, "There are girls in the tournament?"

"Sure," said George, "why not?"

"I'm not playing girls," said Gary.

"Me neither," said Matt.

"Hey, I'm ready," said Tony.

I said to Gary, "You're afraid of getting beat."

"Right," said Gary. "I'm also afraid a rhino will come through that door and steal my court shoes. Give me a break."

Joel said, "We really have to play girls? With these suck T-shirts?"

"Will you guys relax," I said, but I felt the same

way they did. It just made the tournament stupid. It made it feel like a joke.

George told us not to worry and then outlined our offense. He told us who was a guard: me, Tony, Matt, and Gary, and who the posts were: Kent and Joel.

Then he said, "Bring the ball down the court and shoot it in the hoop."

We looked at him in amazement.

Kent said quietly to me, "Is this guy brilliant or what?"

"Or what," I said.

Gary and Matt were fighting. Joel said his face hurt. I didn't have good feelings about this whole thing.

I looked across the gym and my dad was waving to me from the scorers' bench. My grandmother was behind him. She had pom-poms the color of our tanks. Oh, I forgot to say what color that was . . . ugly yellow with black letters. We looked like bumblebees.

7

"ell, guys," I said, "let's take the court. Get this over with."

"Look at them," said Kent.

"Look at them," said Joel.

"I'm in love," said Tony.

The girls had hit the court and were warming up running drills. They were passing, shooting, and making them like nothing we'd ever seen. They knew what they were doing. They had a real coach, a real offense, and they had a pizza place as a sponsor. We were in trouble.

Kent hit me on the head with a ball. "We're in deep Bozo," he said.

"Let's warm up," I said, trying to sound cool and calm. "It'll be a piece of cake. You'll see."

We went out and tried to psych the girls out with some drills of our own. We did this kind of passing drill where you pass and run, that we think makes us look like the Harlem Globetrotters. Except, this time we looked like dirt clods.

Gary tripped right off and floor-burned his knees. He had to do everything he could to keep from crying. I said we'd try another drill. The girls were doing something they called the five-girl weave.

"They look hot," said Tony. "I want to marry the seven-foot wonder."

"Let's just shoot some," said Joel.

"Okay," I said, but then Kent and Tony bumped heads reaching down for the same ball.

"Headache city," said Kent.

The girls were laughing at us. I was trying not to look at them, but they were making their shots, and we might as well have been throwing bricks against the wall.

"Loosen up," I kept saying.

"Right," said Kent, "we're in trouble. Why didn't we practice?"

"We practice all the time," I said.

Then three of the girls did a cheer at us.

They said, "Pick a pack of soda crackers, sis boom dude. Your outfits are ugly and your team is no good."

"They're right," said Gary.

I looked over at George. He was shaking his head and laughing. This wasn't funny.

8

The ref blew the whistle to clear the court. We went over to George. He was still laughing.

"I'll tell you only one thing," said George. "The team that has the most fun wins."

The whole team looked at me.

"Anything else?" I said to our coach.

"Stay out of foul trouble," George said. "You've only got one guy to spare."

I said, "Guys, we've got to boogie. We don't have much time, so we have to get the ball down the court and into the hoop."

"Sounds like a plan," said Matt.

"Pick someone you're dying to defense," said George. He was letting us pick who we'd defense, and it was a big mistake.

Tony said, "I've got to have number three. We're in love and we're going to get married."

George looked at him like he was weird.

"Forget it," I said. "She is two feet taller than you. You couldn't come close to blocking her shot. You'll be too busy looking at her knee pads."

"No," said George. "I think it's good. You have to have a feeling like you want to defense someone."

Tony was pumped.

Gary said, "We're playing girls and we're going to lose. I hate basketball."

George said, "Oh, by the way, Brent, you'll be our captain."

"Gee, thanks," I said, trying to sound like I meant it.

Kent said, "Do we have an offensive plan?"

Joel said, "We are offensive. Have you taken a look at our uniforms?"

George thought that was a real funny one.

"Guys," I said, "we get the ball in the hoop, quickly and often."

Joel said he wanted to sit out first, which was a mistake because he was our tallest guy.

"Okay," I said, "Kent, you and Matt play the key and Gary and I will bring the ball down. Tony, you hit the side."

"Now we're there," said George. "Let's cook."

We put our hands together. I like that feeling. You can feel something running through us. It's power . . . jock power. It's like lightning.

We all said, "Let's party!" and broke.

Kent was going to be jumping against number

three for the tip-off. He heard one of the other girls call her Julie.

"Hi," said Kent, being friendly. "My name is Kent."

"Who cares," she said.

Tony butted in. "Excuse me," he said, "I'm Tony and I'll be defensing you today. Sort of checking you out, get it?"

"Get this, slime ball," she said and pushed him out of the way.

Kent and Tony just looked at her with their mouths open.

The whistle blew. The game started. The tip went up.

We went down. The girls got the ball and us. They made a three-pointer just to start things off right.

Then the girl checking Gary intercepted a pass intended for me and fired the ball down to Julie for the fast break. She made two points. We were down by five. We also weren't sure what hit us.

We were less than three minutes into the game. It was going to be a very short game or a very long one. It depended on which side you were on.

I was determined. Next time down the court we got our act a little bit together and I got the ball into Matt who laid it up and got fouled by number 3. Then one of the girls got excited and threw the ball out of bounds. We took it on the turnover, and I shot a three-pointer to tie up the score.

Kent came over to me. He said, "I don't think I want to be your friend anymore. It's too much stress."

9

We worked our buns off the first and second quarters. I hustled like I'd never hustled in my life. I was also yelling at everyone like a maniac. They were just making such dumb mistakes.

Those stupid girls were making shots I thought were impossible. They out-rebounded us like you wouldn't believe, and that dang number 3 stuffed shots down our throats and out our shoes. I hated her.

They were close but they hadn't killed us completely. They'd get two or three points ahead and then we would catch up. When they finally buzzed the end of the first half we were down by three. We'd held on, but they were acting like they'd just gotten warmed up.

"I'm ready for lunch and a nap," said Gary.

Word had gotten out. There was now a huge crowd watching us. Everyone wanted to see the girls beat us. They thought it would be so funny and great.

Number 3 summed it up as we went off the court. She said, "You guys suck."

George was laughing at us. I couldn't take it anymore.

"George, please don't laugh at us, this isn't funny."

Matt turned to me and yelled, "Would you get off everyone's back. If you yell at me one more time, I'm putting the ball through your face."

"Excuse me for being alive," I said. "We just happen to be losing, and it's because we're playing like jerks."

"We're lousy on the boards," said Joel, who was coming in for Matt. "They've got the height and can jump. We've got to concentrate on position."

George said, "Position is important. Anyone else have something they want to say?"

Everyone wanted to gripe about something.

"I'll tell you," said Gary. "They are in my back pocket. The girl that's on me actually pulled on my shorts."

"Man, they are dirty underneath," said Kent. "I've never been pushed like that by guys."

"I love them all," said Tony. "They're rough. My kind of women."

"You're sickening," said Matt, and he pushed Tony.

Tony raised his fist.

"Whoa," said George, "let's lighten up."

28

Just then my grandmother came over with those stupid pom-poms.

"Boys," she said, "the shirts look great. Keep up the good work. Aren't those girls cute?"

"Right, Grandma," I said.

She left and I turned back to the guys. "We can't lose to these girls."

The buzzer rang to start the second half.

Gary said, "Look, the local TV station is here. We're going to be on the news."

"Where did they come from?" said Joel.

"I'm going to throw up," I said to Kent.

"Why did you get us into this?" Kent said.

George said, "The team that has the most fun will win."

I wanted to stick my tongue out at him.

Time-out
The Girls' Team

Jennifer's Story: *What is the big deal? So what if we're a girls' team playing a boys' team? We're going to beat their smelly socks off.*

10

Do you have any idea how hard it is to be named Jennifer? I know you're thinking I must be very shallow because a name shouldn't be much of a handicap . . . but . . . there are so many Jennifers that it's ridiculous. There are millions of us. You can be anywhere and yell "Jennifer," you don't even have to yell it very loud, and I swear fifty Jennifers will turn around and say "What?"

Were all the parents who named their daughters Jennifer brain dead at the same time? Is it a rule that if you make it through natural childbirth you have to name your daughter Jennifer? Don't parents care? Where is their creativity?

I read somewhere and don't ask me where because I forgot, that Jennifer was the current most common name given to girls. We had finally beat out Mary.

"Whoopee!" I said.

Do you know what it feels like to have the most

common name in the United States? I'll tell you whether you want me to or not because I'm just ragged out about it right now. To be a Jennifer is to be totally normal.

It feels so stupid, boring, normal you could fall asleep just saying our name. When you're flirting with guys, which I've never done and actually have no experience in, but if I did and we were playing "guess my name," it would be over in two seconds flat. They wouldn't even have to try.

They would say, "Is it Mary?"

I'd say, "No."

They'd say, "It's Jennifer."

I'd pretend like they were so intelligent but I'd really want to kill them and I'd say, "How'd you guess?"

All this would take only two seconds maximum and then what are you supposed to do? The conversation would be over. I'd never get to know any guys seriously and I'd never get married. All because my parents named me Jennifer.

People don't think I'm being real about this but I totally am. I mean I care about the homeless and lots of stuff. I just hate having a normal name.

I thought about Cleopatra for a name but I've decided that as soon as I can I'm going to change my name to Sybil. Okay, it's ugly as they come. I don't care, because it's unique. Unique is all that matters.

I want to go through my entire life not meeting

another person with my name. I don't want to be in another classroom where I have to be Jennifer B. or Jennifer One or Jennifer anything because there are sixty million of us. If I meet another Sybil, I'll just change my name again.

Next time I'll make it Medusa. You know, the lady with snakes for hair. She turned everyone to stone. It's a great trick if you ask me.

I'm also a girl jock. That's another thing that kind of ticks me off. In our town, girls are "girl jocks." They aren't just jocks. They are "girl jocks."

It's, like, you can't tell? I mean, maybe when I was three you couldn't tell. However, I'm in the seventh grade now and although I don't have, as my retarded mother says, a "filled-out figure," I don't look anything like a boy.

It didn't matter that I didn't have a "filled-out figure" like some girls I know, who think they are just hot stuff because their hormones managed to kick in, and way too early if you ask me. It didn't matter because the only time anyone ever saw that I had a body was in the summer because the rest of the year I had to wear an ugly, disgusting, retarded school uniform. Yes, folks, I survived Our Lady of Perpetual Sorrow School. The sorrow had to have something to do with looking at those funky school uniforms.

I'm going to go to public school next year. I can't wait. I'm wearing only unique clothing.

11

Well, so what, I'm a girl jock. I'm into sports so somebody shoot me. My goal is to be in the Olympics, I'm not sure which event yet. Then I'm going to be something totally unique like a jockey when I grow older. You know, like a horse racing jockey.

I want to wear those satin blouses and pants and those riding boots. I'll be Sybil the fastest-most-uncommon jockey in the world. I really like horses a lot.

My parents laugh at me because we don't even live near horses, and I've only ridden at camp.

I have this to say to my parents: "Stranger things have happened."

Besides, I tell them they just aren't creative, and to prove my point I remind them that they named me Jennifer, the most common name in the world.

Anyway, back to sports. I like them a lot. I don't know why. I guess what it comes down to is that it feels good to beat people. I mean, I like to compete. But also, wouldn't it feel terrific to sometime just beat the living tar out of certain people you know?

I think I got into sports because you got to wear something besides a plaid wool skirt, white blouse, and a green blazer. That's kind of a cool thing about sports. You wear all these different things, and they are totally comfortable and most of the time cool-looking.

I also like to feel in shape. I like to feel strong. I like to be able to run and stuff and not feel like I'm going to pass out. I think people look better, too, when they're in shape.

I do all sorts of sports. I like swimming and track. I also play volleyball and I'm taking tennis lessons because my dad wants me to. I'm pretty good at tennis but I'm my best at basketball. I was one of the better players at our school, which probably isn't saying much.

I like the feel of the ball in my hands. I totally love the feeling in my stomach when I shoot the ball and it goes through the net. I'm totally amazed when it does. I consider it a miracle.

I like sports because you get to sweat and nobody is totally grossed out about it except maybe my mother.

She says, "Don't call it that. Horses sweat, men perspire, and ladies glow."

I say, "That's pretty weird, Mom."

I sweat and like it.

I ask my mother, "Don't you ever want to be like Jane Fonda and just go for it?"

She says, "Not on TV. Or anywhere people can watch me."

My mom walks to keep her "filled-out figure" not so filled out. She walks and glows.

My mother is sort of like a firefly that way.

My dad and mom think I'm beautiful. It sort of makes up for them naming me you know what. I think my hair is about my best feature. I've got good hair. I'm not being conceited about it. I'm just telling you my best feature.

It is now summer and my best feature has finally grown out of the permanent that my mother, who I will never trust or listen to again, talked me into at the beginning of the year. I have been Jennifer the porcupine-head for nine months. I used to have to force it into braids and hats, anything to hold it down.

I still braid it when I play basketball because it keeps it out of my eyes when I start to glow and also it's turned into this good luck thing. When I'm playing I usually want all the luck I can get.

12

Boys and girls are different. I know you're saying, "No, duh, Jennifer, that's brilliant." That's not what I meant. I know you know the difference between girls and boys because if you don't you're probably in major trouble or dying of terminal geekiness. What I mean is girls who play sports are not like boys who play sports.

Basically, girls realize it's a game. Boys haven't figured it out yet. They're ridiculous.

Boys are always showing off, too. Girls are sensible. We go out and do what needs to be done without being weird.

I think girls like it when people are watching them play and yell things at them and stuff. I mean, not yelling bad stuff. Yelling good stuff like, "You're great. Keep going. Way to go!!" Everyone likes to hear that stuff. However, girls don't go off the deep end about it. They just think it's cool and leave it at that.

Boys, on the other hand, have to go all to pieces

when anyone watches them do anything. I mean, you'd think they were someone super hot by the way they act. They always think it's outstanding when someone watches them, like, playing basketball, but when someone does they go out there and dork out and look stupid.

The harder they try the worse they look. I don't understand it. They are so busy trying to show off and at the same time watch the person watching them. No wonder it doesn't work.

Girls aren't like that. At least the girls on our team aren't like that.

I suppose we have different problems.

I'm on a cool basketball team this summer. We met at a month-long basketball camp at the college in town. It was major fun. It would have been more fun if we could have stayed there at night but we couldn't. It was one of those day camp things.

We still had fun. Mainly because our team was pretty cool and our coach was just exceptional. Her name is Monique. Is that wonderful or what?

I mean, it is so French and cool. She's not French but she could be. She's that cool.

Our team cleaned up at camp. We trounced every team there. We did drills and fundamentals and stuff. Then we would play games against each other.

It was for four hours every morning, which

could get kind of boring. Monique was really good at making it fun. One afternoon she loaded us in her van and we all went shopping. She is so cool.

She was the only coach there that didn't wear a whistle. I think that says a lot. There was this really fat cow that had this other team and they were so lousy and the reason was that she blew her whistle every two seconds.

We called her Coach Moo. Her real name was Ms. Hall. I guess she didn't have a first name. Maybe it was Jennifer and she was too embarrassed to let us know. It would figure.

She drove them crazy. They lost every game, and it's all her fault. One girl was practically in tears. She just hated her coach. I told her to tell her parents to get their money back.

Her team tried to steal the whistle but they didn't have enough energy. She made them do five hundred line drills every second. They didn't have the strength to do anything.

Line drills are these totally exhausting things. You line up at the end of the court and then when the coach blows the whistle you run out to the top of the key and back. Then you run to the middle line of the court and back. You never get to stop or rest. By now you can't breathe and you have to run to the top of the key at the other end of the court and back. Then just when you think you are going to die you have to run to the end of the court and back. The worst is when they time you and you have to beat a certain time or do it all again. It is *total* abuse.

Monique didn't make us do line drills. We did these really strange things, like one day she had us play basketball in roller skates. It was bloody but it was a total riot. You have never seen knee burns like the ones we got.

Heather got totally out of control and rolled into the drinking fountain. She hit it so hard in the stomach that she spit her retainer out and bent it all to crap. It was so sick.

We had this one day where we had to tape our right arms to our sides if we were right-handed and our left arms to our sides if we were left-handed. It was so we would have to dribble with our weakest hand. It was such a disaster. I couldn't do anything.

Then when we took off the tape we died laughing at each other because it pulled every hair off our arms. We were screaming our heads off. Monique kept saying she was sorry but we really didn't care. We were just glad she was making it fun.

It was so lucky we had Monique. It was probably the luckiest thing that happened to me in a long time. Every girl was jealous of our team.

13

I'd better introduce you to the rest of our team. We're all super good friends except one of us. I'll tell you about her later.

Anyway, we're all in sixth, seventh, or eighth grade. The camp was a middle school or junior high level camp. Only one person on our team was in eighth grade, and she is now my very best friend.

Her name is Julie. She is just incredibly tall and beautiful. Everyone tells her she has to be a model. They tell her she just has to.

It is just like her though, she looks at them and says, "I'd rather die."

That's why I like her. She is so cool and beautiful but she isn't stuck up about it at all. She'd rather have fun and do stuff. She's also really smart. She wants to be a marine biologist and do stuff with dolphins. It's so great.

Then there's Heather. She's the youngest on the team. She's in sixth grade. She's the wildest and funniest girl I know. Everybody likes her.

She's into animals big time. She has two dogs, bunnies, birds, fish, and a zillion cats. She's a vegetarian because she doesn't believe in killing animals.

Her dad hates them. Heather says he's really sick. He threatens to kill and eat them all the time.

She's the only girl I know close to our age who has ever dyed her hair. One day, just for fun, she dyed her red hair, jet black. Her mother came home and started hyperventilating. She had to breathe into a paper bag to stop. Heather almost had to call 911. Heather was grounded for life and had to pay her parents back for the fortune they spent at the beauty salon to restore her natural hair color.

Heather said, "I don't know why they just didn't let me grow it out."

Sophia is also on our team. Is Sophia a great name or what? Sophia hates to be called Sophie.

She says Sophia means wisdom.

We said, "Sure, Sophia."

She isn't exactly the wisdom woman. She never understands things. She always asks, "What are you guys talking about?" like she never gets what we're talking about even if it's like how mental our parents are. When someone tells a joke, she always says, "I don't get it."

She's really cute. She's going to my school next

year and we're both in seventh grade. We're going to see if we can't share a locker.

Then there's Maria. She is the smallest on our team. She is so excellent.

She is super fast. She could be a track star tomorrow. She wants to be a ballerina. If she could play basketball with toe shoes she would. She's really into it.

She's playing basketball because her dad made her brother take ballet so he'd be better at soccer. He thought if ballet was good for sports then sports were probably good for ballet. It sounds bizarre to me, too.

Besides being fast she can also jump. It is so weird. She jumps and when she's up in the air her toes are pointed and her arms are, like, doing something exotic. She can't help it. She's had too much ballet.

Those are the five normal people on our team. We all get along. Then there is Natalie.

14

The worst thing to be in the world is a ball hog. Natalie is a ball hog. She snorts she is such a hog.

Nobody likes her on the team and it is her own fault. She is this incredible stuck-up ball hog. You don't even want to be around her.

She thinks she knows everything because her dad is supposed to be this great basketball player and, like, who cares? So she's always telling us what we're doing wrong and telling us to get serious and stuff. We just hate her.

I guess I should tell you what a ball hog is: It's someone who will never pass the ball. They get the ball and they hold onto it. They never let anyone else shoot. Natalie is a total ball hog. She'd shoot from the restroom before she'd stoop so low as to pass the ball to someone else.

Another irritating thing she does is that she crosses herself before she shoots a free throw.

46

You know what crossing yourself is. It's making the sign of the cross on your body.

It is *so* irritating because we know she's not Catholic or even Episcopalian. Julie knows her from her church. Julie says she's a Baptist and Baptists never cross themselves.

We don't know what she's trying to prove except she's trying to look cool. Well, Natalie, it doesn't work at all. You are so not cool it isn't funny.

We're super mean to her, and it's like she thrives on it. The meaner we are the more she likes it. We had this Vaseline thing going for a couple of days.

We put Vaseline on her brush. You wouldn't believe how beautiful and greasy it makes your hair. We put it on the toilet seat just before she used it. Old slime bottom we call it.

She came out and was laughing. She said, "You guys are so funny!"

She thought we were doing things to her because we liked her. We stopped totally.

Maria tried to explain to her that we'd like her to pass the ball every now and then so we could all have a chance to shoot. Well, she still didn't get it. Heather, who is always in a good mood, finally had it and told her she was going to break her arm if she didn't pass to her. Julie told her she'd break her face.

Natalie finally got it and was a little better. At least she passed to Heather and Julie. I didn't want her to pass to me.

Monique was really nice to her. I couldn't understand it. Maybe Monique is nice to everybody. She's cool enough she can pull it off.

We tried to lose Natalie when we went shopping. We told her to try this ugly flowered dress on. When she went into the dressing room we ran out of the store and went to one that was at the other end of the mall. She bought the dress and found us. She's such a ball hog.

15

Julie called me.

"Monique wants us to be in a tournament," she said.

"A tournament?" I asked.

"Yes," said Julie, "it's a city thing and there are prizes and stuff."

"What kind of stuff?" I asked.

Julie said, "Give me a break. I don't know. Probably trophies. Does it matter?"

"I just kind of wondered. I was hoping it would be something cool like jackets or something, or maybe gift certificates. That would be cool."

"That's if we win," said Julie.

"We have to win," I said, "what team could there be that we haven't already wiped up on?"

"Get this," said Julie, "it's really a boys' tournament. Monique thinks we'll be the only girls' team there."

"We're going to play boys?" I asked.

"We're going to pulverize boys," said Julie.

"What a kick. What if we win the tournament?"

"Why are we in a boys' tournament?"

"I guess Monique found out about it and tried to get them to set up a girls' tournament along with it, but they said they didn't have time. She said well then they had to let us play, and they said they'd think about it, and they thought about it and let us in."

"I've never played against boys," I said. "Boys' rules?"

"Ya," said Julie. "We're going to practice. We've got a couple of weeks. We'll get it down no problem."

"Okay," I said. "Is everyone doing it?"

"Ya," said Julie, "we have to have six team players to enter."

"That means . . ."

"Ball hog!" we both screamed.

"So do you think you know any of these guys?" I asked.

"I hope not," she said. "Wait. I take it back. It might be fun to get back at some of the twerps I've gone to school with."

I got off the phone and told my mother that I was going to be in a boys' basketball tournament.

She said, "Isn't that different."

My dad thought it was great.

My mom said, "You'll be playing against boys?"

"Yes, Mother," I said.

"Well, are you old enough, dear?" she asked.

"Mother, it isn't a date. It's a game," I said.

"Well, isn't that different," she said again.

I looked at her like she was insane.

"Honey, I don't like the way you're looking at me."

I can't wait till I'm Medusa. I may skip Sybil.

16

We practiced every day for two weeks. We were looking pretty good. We were realistic though. We knew our competition was going to be better than anything we'd played against.

Everyone had improved and sort of had her specialty. I had pretty much perfected this shot outside the key on either side that Monique said would come in handy. For some reason I could make the thing in my sleep.

One day we all put basketballs under our shirts to see what we'd look like pregnant. Heather took our picture and made copies. My mom didn't think it was all that funny.

We worked out this great warm-up routine. Monique says it would be to psych out the other team. We ran around and did this wild routine passing the ball. It looked like we didn't know where it was going, but we had it all worked out like a dance, and it looked really good if I say so myself.

"Look hot," she said, "and the battle will be half over."

Ballet is really good for dribbling and making moves toward the basket. Maria can do these incredible things and drive to the basket without losing control once. Of course she does it with her toes pointed.

One day Monique talked these guys that were hanging around into playing us. It wasn't really fair because they were younger than us and they weren't really a team. I mean, they didn't have someone telling them what offense to run and what sort of pattern to work in order to get someone in the open so they could shoot.

We murdered them and it felt great. Monique had to buy them ice cream and pop so they wouldn't be big baby losers. Guys can be so weird.

They kept saying, "You guys are just lucky."

Julie said, "Lucky smucky. We're good."

Monique said, "Now there's only one thing a good woman needs to do before she goes to a tournament."

"What's that?" said Sophia.

"Which word don't you understand?" asked Heather.

"You guys," she said. "I get it. I just wonder what we have left to do."

We all looked at Monique and she looked at us.

"Girls — we have to have something new to wear. We have to go shopping!"

"Uniforms," said Natalie. "We have to have uniforms."

She said it like she loved them.

"Monique," I said, "I've got this thing against uniforms."

"That's why you have to go pick them out. We won't stop shopping till everyone is happy."

Heather said, "Can we get scooped necks instead of V necks? My mom says I look funny in a V neck."

I said, "Okay, I'll wear one as long as it isn't wool plaid and a blazer."

Julie said, "You're so weird."

17

Monique had gotten us a sponsor. It was a pizza place. Julie said that was cool.

The only requirement was we had to use their colors, which were red and gold. We also had to put their name on our backs. Our shirts had to say "The Pizza Place" on them.

Honestly, I would be thrilled with anything that wasn't green plaid. I wouldn't care what they said — as long as they didn't have one thing on them: our names.

"Are they going to have our names?" I asked.

"Not unless you all want them," Monique said.

We voted and nobody wanted her name on them. It was a relief. If we were going to put names on I was going to put Sybil. I'd tell my parents it was just misspelled.

Shopping was easy. We picked out the shirts first. Yes, we got scooped necks so Heather's mom would be happy. Then we matched shorts.

Monique really picked everything out. She's so good at it though, why would you argue?

The guy putting the letters and numbers on was a little ticked that it had to be this rush order, but Monique explained that we were late entering the tournament. He wanted to know which tournament and Monique told him.

"What are you doing playing in a boys' tournament?" he asked.

Monique didn't answer him. "Do you want the order or not?" she said.

He said, "It isn't like the good old days."

"I'm glad," said Monique.

We got out of the store and Julie asked Monique, "What is the big deal really? Who cares who we play?"

"People are weird," said Monique. "People are weird."

"It's just a game," I said. "It's just for fun."

Sophia said, "What? What are you guys talking about?"

We got our shirts and shorts the day before the tournament. Socks were a problem but Monique found some that matched perfectly. I hit my parents up for new shoes but they were against it.

I couldn't believe it when it was the day of the tournament. I couldn't believe my parents were going, even my mother.

She said, "I want to see what you've been doing with all your time."

I got to the gym and everyone but Sophia was there. Monique showed us to our locker room. She said that since we were girls, we were the only ones with a permanent locker room, at least till we lost.

We went in and got changed. I was the only one that hadn't brought tons of makeup to put on. I felt totally left out.

Julie said, "Use mine, I've got plenty."

"Do your eyes," said Maria, "and spray your hair so it isn't out of control."

I put on just a touch of eye shadow. I didn't do anything too wild. I didn't need to spray my hair. I'd put my hair up in braids. I did it for luck.

Maria then proceeded to spray her hair and got spray in Heather's eye. Her eye needed more than makeup. It looked like it needed surgery. She had to wash it out about six hundred times.

Sophia came in, and was tearing her bag apart. I said, "Sophia, what are you doing?"

"I lost my underwear," she said.

"You're not wearing any?" I said. I was totally amazed.

"Of course I am, stupid! I've lost my lucky underwear to wear in the game."

At this point, Natalie the ball hog was standing in front of the mirror being a mirror hog. She was using an entire can of hair spray on her hair. Her head looked like she was wearing a brown bicycle helmet.

"How does it look?" asked Natalie.

"Like a bicycle helmet," said Julie.

"Oh, good," said Natalie.

Sophia got out her perfume and started spraying. We had to open the outside door.

Monique came in, took one whiff, looked at Natalie's hair, Heather's eye, and said, "Well, I guess we're ready."

At that point, this total geek boy with a ponytail came in. He took one look at us and freaked. He ran out of the room like a racehorse.

"What's his problem?" said Julie.

Monique said, "We play Granny's Antiques first. I've met their coach. We have nothing to worry about."

We all got in a circle and hugged each other. We even included Natalie. I kind of felt like crying. We were the Girl Jocks. It was cool.

Monique said, "Dazzle them, *girls*. Let's have some fun."

18

We hit the court. Our parents started yelling. They were totally pumped and so were we.

Monique said, "Act like it's a practice. Have fun."

We started running our drills. It was fantastic. We could do nothing wrong.

Only one thing happened. Sophia accidentally hit Natalie in the head with the ball but, with Natalie's hair spray helmet on, it bounced right off.

"Look at the team we're playing," said Julie.

I looked just as two guys were reaching down to pick up the same ball and hit heads. I noticed this cute guy. I heard one of the other guys call him Brent.

I thought, Great, he's got an unusual name.

"Look at those alien uniforms," said Heather.

Sophia said, "What does it mean, 'Get old at Granny's'?"

Julie, Heather, and Maria had gone over toward

the boys and said a little cheer about their uniforms. I couldn't believe they did it.

Julie said, "It will psych them out."

The referee blew the whistle to clear the court. Monique went over the rules one more time, to make sure there weren't any questions. Guess who had one?

"Which basket is ours?" asked Sophia.

"Listen to me carefully, Sophia," said Julie, "the basket we have been practicing at is ours. Shoot only at that one until halftime."

"I got it," said Sophia.

Then I don't know what got into me.

I said, "Natalie, don't hog the ball."

She didn't stick her tongue out or anything. She just said, "Okay."

We broke and went to mid-court for the jump ball. Julie was talking to the guy she was jumping against. Then this other guy came up and she had to put her hand up like she was trying to keep him from getting any closer. The guy was this total geek. Everyone was yelling so I couldn't hear what they were saying.

I looked over and saw TV cameras. I couldn't believe it. We were going to be on TV.

The referee said, "Let's play basketball" and blew his whistle. The game started. I thought I was going to throw up.

The tip went up and Julie totally controlled the ball. She fired it over to Natalie. Natalie, of course, shot even though she was eight miles away. The good thing was she made it. The other good thing was that it was so far away that it was a three-pointer.

Then Maria stole the ball. It was amazing. She threw it as hard as she could to Julie. Julie made an easy trip to the basket, and we were in the lead by five points.

We were nuts. I guess we then got a little too excited. Julie got a foul. Then Maria accidentally threw the ball out of bounds.

It seemed like we all looked at Monique at once.

She yelled, "You're doing fine. Relax. Enjoy yourself. Run the offense."

We did. We sort of settled down and Julie got incredibly hot. I mean she couldn't miss a shot.

You know what? I no longer felt like throwing up. I was having fun. It was cool. I even made two baskets.

We pretty much stayed ahead of the boys for the first two quarters. It wasn't by a lot but we were still ahead. At the buzzer for the first half we were leading by three.

We went back into the locker room at halftime. Sophia found her missing underwear and put them on. She was very relieved. We told her no more perfume.

Natalie asked what her hair looked like.

"Cement," I said.

"Great," she said.

19

We were starting the second half.

I said to Julie, "This is sure going fast."

She said, "I know. Isn't it fun?"

"Ya," I said.

"Do you think any of the guys are cute?" I asked.

"Ya, sort of," said Julie. "I like the guy with the muscles."

"He's cute," I said.

"Who do you like?" she asked.

I said, "I kind of like Brent."

"Which one is he?" she said.

I pointed him out.

"Oh, he's cute, too. He's too short for me. You can keep him."

We both laughed.

Sophia was standing in the middle of the floor rearranging her underwear.

Julie said, "Sophia, everyone plus the TV cameras is watching you fix your undies. Are you happy?"

Sophia looked at us like she didn't understand a word we were saying.

She said, "They're kind of old and the elastic is loose."

"Maybe you should go change," I said.

"It'll be okay," she said, but she was still digging in her pants trying to pull the legs down. "They're for good luck."

"Well, good luck," I said.

Julie ran over and got a drink. We went over to our bench and the buzzer sounded. Monique said to get in a circle.

We put our arms around each other again.

Monique said, "I'm so proud of you girls. You're playing so well . . . and . . . you all look just fantastic!"

We all laughed and gave each other a group hug. The referee said, "Let's play ball."

I looked over at my parents. They were waving at me. My mom even looked like she was enjoying herself. I wondered what she thought of all this glowing.

We started the third quarter. We were still doing great, making shots. We were also staying ahead. I could tell the guys were flipping out. Being beat by the girls wasn't something they looked forward to.

We were having a slight problem with Natalie. She was starting to boss people around. She'd point her finger at you like you were supposed to go that direction and she'd say things.

She'd bark like a dog, "Defense."

It was embarrassing.

She was also starting to hog the ball, but Julie told her that nobody would pass to her if she was going to be a ball hog.

Right before a foul shot Maria zoned out a little and forgot where she was and did a pirouette. The crowd went nuts. It was kind of cool.

I was really enjoying myself. I realize now I didn't want to win just for the prize or just because people would think you were hot stuff. I wanted to win so Julie, Maria, Heather, Sophia, Natalie, and I could keep playing together. We were the Girl Jocks and we were proud of it.

Time-out
The Boys' Team

Brent: *This can't be happening. Where did these girls come from? Why are they picking on us?*

20

I think our problem is feet," said Joel. "We need to work on our sense of balance — our connection with gravity."

"Don't start in," said Tony.

We were heading out to the floor and number 3 was beside us returning from the drinking fountain. When she thought no one was looking she accidentally rammed her foot down on top of Kent's.

"Oh, sorry," she said.

"My problem is feet, all right," said Kent. "She's spent more time on my shoes than I have. She might as well wear them. I'm going to get her."

"You can't hit a girl," I said.

"I'm not going to," said Kent. "I'm going to make her eat a basketball."

"What is Tony doing now?" I asked.

He was over by number 33. He was saying something to her. Then it looked like she was shoving the basketball into his nose.

He came back with one hand pinching his nostrils shut and the other cupped under it.

"I have a bloody nose," he said.

"We have to think about our feet," said Joel. "Basketball is about balance and gravity. We have to think about gravity."

"Joel," said Gary, "please don't talk about gravity anymore."

"She hates me," said Tony. "She doesn't even know me and she hates me."

He went over to the bench to find a towel.

One of the refs said, "Are you going to play or what?"

"We're coming," I said.

Joel whispered to me, "Think gravity."

I said, "Joel, don't get weird. You can't get weird. Think baskets."

We controlled the tip-off and were bringing the ball downcourt. Gary bounced it off his foot and it went out of bounds.

"Smooth move," said Matt, who came in for Tony.

"Let's see you do better," said Gary.

The girls had the ball, took a shot but then bricked it. I grabbed the rebound, pumped a pass to Joel, and number 33 intercepted it.

"Can't you catch anything?" I said.

"Can't you pass anything?" he said.

They made another two points. The crowd yelled. They loved them.

"We're going to lose," said Matt as he left the floor so Tony could come back in.

"My nose look okay?" he asked.

"Give me a break," said Kent.

Joel said, "We aren't thinking about gravity."

"Get the ball in the hoop," I screamed at them.

"Why don't you try it," said Gary.

The ref said, "Do you guys want to fight with each other or do you want to play basketball?"

We played basketball, sort of. I couldn't breathe. I couldn't shoot. I hated to lose. I just hate to lose.

21

We fought each other and the girls through the third quarter and into the fourth. There were three minutes to be played in the game. I was passing the ball in bounds.

Gary took it downcourt. This really cute girl with the braids was right with him. He passed it to Joel. The whistle blew. Kent got called for three seconds in the key.

We all stood in the middle of the floor and screamed. We were nuts.

"Uncle" George finally decided to call a time-out.

"What's going on?" he said.

"They are," said Matt, "and on and on."

"Okay, guys," he said, "now we're going to play my game."

"What do you mean?" I said without an ounce of respect.

Tony was picking at his bloody nose. I wanted to bash it in.

"Huddle up," said George. "Get your arms around each other."

"Guys," I said and I put my arms around Joel and Kent. They put their arms around Matt and Gary. Tony then squeezed in.

"I don't think we're the Jocks anymore," said Tony.

"Knock it off," I said.

"No," said George, "you knock it off. He's hit the nail on the head. You guys stink, and it's because you've forgotten why you're together and why you're here."

"I don't get it," said Gary.

"It's simple, jerks," said George. "You guys like each other. You like to have fun together. The reason you're here is to have fun."

"We're not having fun," said Kent.

"No, you're not," said George, "and if you haven't noticed, the girls are having a heck of a good time."

"And they're also winning," I said.

George said, "Which comes first? The chicken or the egg?"

"You mean," said Joel, "do you have a good time first and then win or do you win and then have a good time?"

George said, "I'll say it for the last time. The team that has the most fun wins."

It was like I was hit by lightning. I got it. George wasn't totally weird.

"Let's party," I screamed.

We went back out onto the court. The air had changed. George was a geek but we knew he was right.

I said to Kent, "Why not? Win or lose, it's time to have some fun. I'm sorry for yelling at everyone."

Joel said, "I was wrong. It's not gravity. It's attitude."

"Check it at the door," I said.

Matt said, "The good-time jocks have hit the floor."

Kent went over to number 33 and flexed his biceps at her. "Check this out," he said.

I waved at Braids.

Tony asked one of the girls if she wanted to look up his nostrils. The girls looked at us like we were crazy.

We were crazy. We were crazy to forget why we played basketball. We played because it was fun.

First off Gary stole the ball from Braids and fired it to Joel who made two points with a lay-in. He was fouled in the process and made both shots on a one-and-one. We were only three points down with two minutes to go.

Matt said, "We can win."

Kent said, "Who cares, let's have a good time."

The girls got called for walking against our full

court press. Their coach was coming unglued. We had the ball.

"Keep laughing," I said.

"You're crazy or stupid," said Braids.

"Both," I said laughing. Then I popped in a three-pointer. We were tied.

The girls took the ball downcourt. Then they passed it to the girl Tony was checking, and he asked her again if she wanted to look up his nostrils. She threw the ball at him. He happily took it and headed down the court.

"Best bloody nose I've ever had," he said.

He passed it to Gary who worked it into Kent. Kent went up for the shot and was fouled by our old friend number 33. There were three seconds left in the game.

As he went to the foul line he said to her, "This is on your foot."

He made the first shot and we went nuts. We were ahead. He missed the second shot but it was too late for the girls. They tried to shoot from midcourt but they didn't even come close.

We won.

"Nothing like a good time," I said.

Time-out
The Girls' Team

Jennifer: *What has happened to the boys? We're falling apart. I wonder if my mother can tell how much makeup I have on?*

22

What happened? We were so hot and then things just kind of fell apart. With three minutes left in the game we had them. We were totally nailing them to the wall.

We made a couple of mistakes. I got the ball stolen from me and it really ticked me off. Nothing is more maddening. It's like your brain doesn't get that you've now lost the ball and you want to keep going. You feel like a complete fool.

The only thing I can figure is something happened to the boys. They finally called a time-out. They really needed it, too. Their tallest guy got called for three seconds in the key and they all stood in the middle of the court and screamed like crazy people. Didn't I tell you that guys, like, take it so seriously?

They went to their bench and I guess their coach finally got them going or something. They came back and it was a major shift in attitude. I'm not being conceited but they came back onto the floor and started playing more like we were.

It was, like, all of a sudden they decided it was a game. They were being totally weird but they were at least having fun.

Heather said that this geek kept asking her, "Do you want to look up my nostrils?"

She had no idea where he was coming from. Isn't that about the sickest thing you've ever heard? She got so grossed out that she threw the ball at him.

"Take that," she said and she attempted to pass the ball up his nose.

It was a major boo-boo. It wasn't bad that she threw the ball at him. It was bad that he managed to grab the ball and get it down the court and score.

Natalie then decided to you know what: ball hog. She thought we needed her excellent help. She decided she was a one-woman team.

"I'm going to strangle her," said Julie. "Don't try to stop me."

"I wouldn't think of it," I said.

Natalie couldn't get near the basket so she stood around dribbling.

In front of everyone I went up to her and said, "Stop dribbling. You are acting like an idiot."

She stopped but it wasn't soon enough.

Julie fouled and the guys went to the foul line with three seconds left and the score tied.

Julie said, "Come on, it isn't over yet."

However, it was. The guy made the first shot. He missed the second but by the time we got the ball, I should say Natalie got the ball, and shot from midcourt and of course missed, the game was over.

Maria was closest to me and hugged me.

"Winning isn't everything, is it?" she said.

"Losing isn't everything, is it?" I said.

Natalie started crying.

Julie said, "I swear I'm going to give her something to cry about."

She didn't. She went up to her and she put her arms around her.

23

Monique was disappointed.
She said, "You girls are wonderful. You played a great game. You looked beautiful. You still look beautiful. I'm so proud of you."

We knew she meant it. We also knew she was disappointed. Well, so were we.

We were out of the tournament. It was a one day single elimination tournament. We'd lost our chance.

Julie said, "There'll be other tournaments."

Sophia decided she was never going to wash her uniform. She was going to keep it just the way it was.

"I want to remember this team forever," she said.

"Insane," said Julie. "It smells."

"Wash it," I said. "Remember us clean."

"Oh, you guys," she said.

We tried watching the rest of the tournament

with Monique but it was a drag. It's just not the same when you've lost out.

Heather talked Natalie into letting her draw a tattoo on her arm with a pen. She told her she would look just like Cher. Natalie didn't. She looked like a girl with hair like a bicycle helmet that had let Heather draw on her arm with a pen.

We went for salads between games. We came back in and watched a little while longer. Julie and I snuck out.

There was a bookstore across the street. We went in. I bought this book that Julie said was really good. It's called, *You, Me, and Gracie Makes Three*. I've just started it but I love it.

We went back to the gym and watched the Granny's get wiped. It served them right. They were out of the tournament now, too.

Sophia said, "Wouldn't it be just too weird if they, like, came up and sat by us."

They didn't.

After all the games we went to our sponsors for dinner. We went to the Pizza Place. It was great.

First we played every song we hated on the jukebox. Every time we heard a new song we tried to guess who picked it. They had "Happy Birthday" on the jukebox and I picked it.

"What song is this?" said Sophia.

"It's 'Happy Birthday,' " said Julie.

"Really?" said Sophia.

Then we took over the pay phone. We were organizing a sleepover for all of us. We knew it would take some major calling to find a parent that would let us all come over.

Our pizzas arrived and Monique told us to stop trying. She invited us to her place. She is so cool.

We were almost done eating and you'll never guess who came in. Granny's team walked in the door.

"I still think that guy is cute," I said to Julie.

Julie wrote something on a napkin and threw it on their table.

"What did you write?" I asked.

"I just told him how much you loved him."

I died.

"You didn't?" I said.

She laughed at me.

I said, "I'm going to kill you if you did."

We decided to give them a special present. We called the waiter over and pooled all our money together. Monique even kicked in some money because she thought it was funny.

"No use in being a poor sport," she said.

Time-out
The Boys' Team

Brent: *Winning isn't everything. Win or lose it's how you play the game.*
  The Jocks still like to win.

24

We won that game. We didn't win the tournament. We did have fun though.

Hey, we weren't stupid. Once we learned what was wrong it didn't take us too long to fix it. We had a blast in our second game.

It was a relief to play guys, let me tell you, and they were normal-sized. They were Wayne's Auto Parts. They had uglier T-shirts than us and they didn't know what had hit them.

We had fifteen points on them the first half and pretty much kept it in the second, finishing the game with a twelve-point lead. I made a couple of my more amazing moves and eleven points. If I do say so myself, I wasn't bad.

Our third game was another story. We were still having fun but I think we were getting a little tired. Winning takes a lot out of you. I'm just kidding.

Kent said we ate too much lunch and too much

protein. He had told us to stick to complex carbohydrates.

I said, "I don't want complex anything. I want
food."

"Eat spaghetti," he said, "and salad."

"Okay," I said as I ate my second hamburger.

I told Tony not to eat the bean burrito. I said,
"You'll regret it. I've had it before."

The game just got started and he came up to
me and said, "I have to go to the bathroom big
and bad if you get my drift."

"Just hold it," I said. "You'll break our rhythm.
We're starting to click."

"I'm going to do more than click," he said, and
he kind of hobbled off the floor.

In the middle of the game the refs ran into each
other and knocked each other down. It was pretty
funny. They had to call a time-out because one of
them was dizzy. I thought he was dizzy before he
got knocked down.

The game was going down the tubes and Kent
came up and asked me if I thought his calves were
getting bigger.

I said, "I don't know. I guess so."

He seemed happy but we lost. Not big time,
but we lost. We were out of the tournament then
but depending on who won the championship
game, we could place as high as fourth. That made
my dad happy.

My grandma came over when the game ended. She hugged me.

"Grandma," I said, "please don't hug me in front of everyone."

"Knock it off," she said, "or I'll kiss you."

She took us out for pizza.

We were just sitting down and Kent said, "I never want to see those girls again."

A napkin landed on our table. On it was a note. We looked over to where it came from. The girls were there eating pizza. Number 33 had sent the note.

It said, "You guys still suck."

We looked at her and she waved.

"Boys," my grandmother said, "you be nice to those young ladies. They risked a lot entering that tournament. They also almost beat the socks off you."

Tony said, "I think we should ask them to join us."

"No way," we all said.

Kent said, "You do and I'm leaving."

He didn't have to because right then the girls all got up to leave.

"See you around," I said to the girl with the braids.

She said, "I hope so," and I almost died right there.

They were out the door and the waiter came

over and brought us a pitcher of what looked like mud water.

He said, "The girls bought this for you."

"What is it?" asked Matt and Gary at the same time.

"They said it was your favorite, root beer and tomato juice."

"Gross," I said and we just looked at it for a while.

Finally Matt said, "We can't let it go to waste."

We had a contest to see who could drink the most without throwing up. No one threw up. Are we amazing or what?

As Joel says, "The Jocks puke for no one, not even girls."

Don't you just love sports?

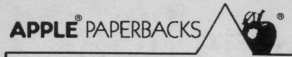